A PICNIC WITH BERT

by WILLIAM VAN HORN

SCHOLASTIC INC.
New York Toronto London Auckland Sydney

To
Mattie Litch
Stan Cohen
Paul Gaertner
and
Larry Darling—

Four teachers who made
all the difference.

ISBN 0-590-32978-2

Copyright © 1983 by William Van Horn.
All rights reserved. Published by Scholastic Inc.

12 11 10 9 8 7 6 5 4 3   0 1 2/9
                                              11

Printed in the U.S.A.

Contents

The Spooky Buzz

Every spring Charlie the dinosaur and his
older brother Fred did their spring-cleaning.
Charlie's job was to clean the house.
Fred's job was to clean the yard.

One day Charlie was washing the windows.
Suddenly, he heard a noise.
"What's that?" he said.
He listened. There it was again!
It was an awful buzzing noise.

Charlie ran outside to get Fred.
But he could not find him anywhere.
Charlie was afraid to go back into the
house alone. So he went to get his
cousin Bert, who lived nearby.

Charlie told Bert about the spooky buzz.
"Let's go!" said Bert, and they hurried
back to Charlie's house.

There was Fred, standing in the yard.
"Where were you just now?" said Charlie.
"I needed you. I heard a strange noise
in the house."

"Really?" said Fred. "What kind of noise?"

"An awful buzzing noise," said Charlie.
"It was spooky, and it scared me."

Fred opened the door slowly.

"I don't hear any noise," he said.
"Do you, Bert?"

"Nope!" said Bert. "I don't hear anything."

Fred laughed.
"You must have been daydreaming, Charlie."

The next day Charlie heard the noise again.
He ran outside —
but Fred was not there.
Charlie had to go get Bert again.

When they returned, they ran
smack into Fred.
"Why do you keep running off, Charlie?"
said Fred. "You'll never get the
housecleaning done that way."

"I heard the buzzing noise again,"
said Charlie.
"It sounds just like a giant bee!"

Fred and Bert stood still and listened.
They didn't hear a thing.
"I think you've got a giant bee
in your brain, Charlie." Fred laughed.

Charlie did not think it was funny.

When he heard the noise on the
third day, Charlie was ready.
"I'm not dreaming," he said.
"This time I'll find out what
that buzzing is all by myself."

Slowly he walked toward the noise.
It was coming from the hall closet.

Charlie tiptoed up to the door.
"Oh, I hope it's *not* a giant bee,"
he whispered.
Carefully, he opened the door. . . .

"Some bee!" said Charlie.
He poked Fred with the broom.
Fred sat up and rubbed his eyes.
"How did you find me?" he asked.

"I heard you snoring," said Charlie.
"*You* were the spooky buzzing noise!"

"Me? Snoring?"
Fred laughed.
"Don't be silly, Charlie.
I never snore!"

But from then on, when Charlie heard a buzzing noise, he knew there was nothing spooky about it.

A Picnic with Bert

One warm summer day,
Fred and Charlie packed a picnic basket
and went to get their cousin Bert.

"We know a great place for a picnic,"
said Fred. "Come with us!"

"We'll swim," said Charlie.

"We'll hike," said Fred.

"What about eat?" said Bert. "Will we eat?"

"Of course we'll eat," said Fred.
"That's what picnics are all about."

When they got to the picnic grounds,
Charlie ran to the pool and dived in.
Fred dived in after him.
But Bert just stood there and
looked at the water.

"Come on in, Bert," said Fred.
Bert shook his head.
"I'm too big to swim," he said.

"No, you're not," said Fred.
"Come on — jump in!"

Bert got ready and got set,
and in he went!

"See?" said Bert. "I told
you I was too big to swim."

"Never mind," said Charlie.
"We can still go for a hike."
Fred led the way to Lookout Hill.
But Bert looked up at the hill and said,
"I'm too big to climb."

"No, you're not," said Fred. "Anybody
can climb. Come on — it's easy."

It was not easy. . . .
But with a little help —

Bert made it all the way to the top.
"Now what?" said Bert.

"Now we go back down," said Fred.
"It's much faster than coming up."

This time Fred was right.

Bert slipped and slid...

and
down
they
went.

"Where are we?" said Charlie.

"I don't know," said Fred.
"I think we're lost."

Bert laughed.
"Maybe you guys are lost—
but I'm not!"

"What do you mean?" said Charlie.

"I'm too big to get lost," said Bert.

With that, Bert began to plow
his way through the bushes.
Charlie and Fred were right behind.

Soon they were all back at the picnic grounds.
"Let's eat!" said Charlie. "I'm starved!"

"Me too," said Fred.

"Me too," said Bert.
"I may be too big to do a lot of things,
but I'm never too big to eat!"

Up, Up, and Away!

Charlie and Fred were watching
some small dinosaurs at play.

Fred bent down.
He waved his arms back and forth—
and up he went.

"Great going, Fred," said Charlie.
"You're doing a bang-up job so far."

"Very funny," said Fred. "That jump
didn't count, anyway. It's just for practice.
Now I'll show you a real jump.
I call it the grasshopper special."

Fred picked out a small bush.
He took a running start—
up he went—

and *splash*!

Charlie smiled. "Maybe you'd better forget
about grasshoppers, Fred, and stop
before you hurt yourself."

But Fred wasn't ready to quit.
"Those jumps were too easy," he said.
"What I really need is something very high
to jump over. The higher I jump,
the farther I go."

"How about that hedge?" said Charlie.
"It's pretty high."

"Okay," said Fred. "But first, go and see
if there's any water on the other side."

Charlie looked through the hedge.
"No water here," he called.

"Good!" said Fred. "Here goes!"
Fred took a running start—
jumped all the way over the hedge—

and landed smack on the back
of a sleeping triceratops.

The big dinosaur was so scared
it began to run.
"Whoa!" cried Fred. "Stop!"

The triceratops didn't stop,
and the more Fred yelled,
the faster it ran.

Many hours later, Fred came back.
Charlie was waiting.
"Well, Fred," he said, "you certainly
went far! And now there's just one
more jump that you have to do today."

"What kind of jump is that?" said Fred.

"A jump into a nice hot bath," said Charlie.
"Come on—it's time to go home."